The Anaconda from Drumcondra

DON CONROY

POOLBEG
FOR CHILDREN

For Justine

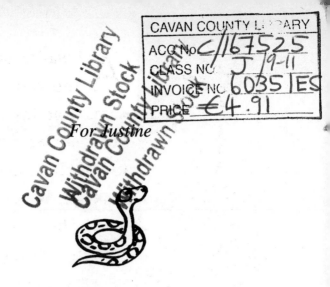

Published 1997
by Poolbeg Press Ltd
123 Baldoyle Industrial Estate
Dublin 13, Ireland

Reprinted November 1997
Reprinted December1998
Reprinted May 2000

© Don Conroy 1997

The moral right of the author has been asserted.

The Publishers gratefully acknowledge the support of The Arts Council.

A catalogue record for this book is available from the British Library.

ISBN 1 85371 876 9

Illustrations by Don Conroy
Cover design by Poolbeg Group Services Ltd
Set by Poolbeg Group Services Ltd in Times 15/21
Printed by The Guernsey Press Ltd,
Vale, Guernsey, Channel Islands.

Al was an anaconda and they say he came from Drumcondra, but there were rumours he had come from foreign parts. Some said he was hot property that had fallen off the back of a lorry.

It was Fred the Ted who first found him twisting and wriggling along the streets and brought him home. Fred was a Teddy boy who always dressed like one, combed his oily hair like Elvis, his idol, wore sideburns and drainpipe trousers. He lived alone in a flat in Drumcondra. He tried to look tough, as Teddy boys should, but in fact he was a softie with a big heart.

1

Although Fred's landlord didn't allow pets, Fred had kept Al well hidden. He bought some plate glass and made a case for Al to live in, even filled it half full with water and put a few water plants in it and a smooth rock the size of a football. It wasn't long before Al settled in.

Fred soon introduced Al to music. Elvis was his favourite, which pleased Fred no end. Sometimes Al would slide in and out of the vinyl and pick his own LP, or EP, as the case may be. Ricky Nelson was popular and, of course, Buddy Holly, not to mention the Everley Brothers, Eddie Cochrane and

Cliff Richard, the most popular '50s singers in Fred's book. Sometimes, when the weather was bad or Fred was feeling a bit blue, there was nobody better to listen to than another of their favourites, Roy Orbison.

They went to the cinema at least three times a week. Al would check out the entertainment page in the evening paper. If there was a good Western film, especially if John Wayne was in it, they'd go to it. It might be as far away as the Stella in Mount Merrion or the De Luxe in Camden Street. Fred would leave early and walk to the cinema, carrying Al around his neck like a scarf. Nobody ever noticed Al, or if they did they said nothing. On the way home, they usually got a one-and-one – fish and chips. Fred preferred smoked cod while Al always asked for fresh cod.

Once, when Fred went to a Saturday

matinee, he carried Al in a bag. He knew the kids would quickly spot him and there would be ructions. Well, as they watched a film called *Swiss Family Robinson,* what did Al see, as large as life on the screen, only the largest snake ever! It was called an anaconda and it was busy trying to squeeze the life out of three actors. Al looked at Fred, who was looking at Al's skin pattern, which was exactly like the giant snake's in the picture. Al could see the blood drain from Fred's face. Fred went very silent and didn't speak for a long time after. They went into a café and Fred sat silently drinking tea.

Al explained it was only a movie and everything looks bigger and gets

4

exaggerated in them. This seemed to calm Fred somewhat, but Al noticed he had gone through several packets of cigarettes by the time they got home. Fred suggested Al sleep in the bath; he said it would be more roomy. Al checked himself in the bathroom mirror. He had to admit  the pattern of his skin was similar to the anaconda's in the film. It was probably all trick photography, he consoled himself. And he wasn't the length of Fred's drainpipe trousers. No, there was no way he could be an anaconda.

Yet Fred the Ted took to locking his bedroom door after that, and made sure Al was always well fed with ham or sardine sandwiches. Al certainly had no objection to that. After a few weeks, things got back to normal. Fred stopped locking his bedroom door and Al had the freedom of the flat again.

Al was soon invited to join Fred the Ted and his buddies for card games up the laneway. There was Gerry the Panda, who always dressed in black and white and waved his arms all the time, Billy the Conker (on account of his bulbous nose), Pockets Pearce, who never seemed to be short of a few bob, and Vinny the Grip, who had a handshake like a vice. Al was asked to sit out at first. Later, he got to know all the games. Poker was the most popular.

One evening, Fred the Ted went to a dance in the Crystal. There he met the girl of his dreams. Her name was Teresa and she was from Glasnevin. Fred discovered that she loved to jive, go to the pictures and listen to music. When he found out she loved Elvis things could not have been better.

Al realised something was up with Fred the Ted. He began to act differently. All he wanted was to listen to love songs. He stopped taking Al to the movies, and bought a portable black-and-white television instead. Al didn't mind, he enjoyed watching this new magic box in the corner.

Then Fred arrived home one evening and

he seemed to be floating on cloud nine. Al knew it was the sign of someone in love. Fred put Teresa's picture on the mantelpiece and began to sing an Elvis song to it.

"Guess what?" said Fred. "Today is a very special day."

Al looked puzzled. "What's so special about Thursday?"

"It's no ordinary Thursday. It's St Valentine's Day. The one day a year set aside for lovers."

"It's been St Valentine's Day every day since you met Teresa," Al retorted.

"I know," beamed Fred. "Listen, Al, no offence, but I've asked Teresa to come over for dinner tonight. I ordered a Chinese take-away." Then he produced a tiny black box and flicked over the lid. "What do you think?" he asked.

"I think it's a diamond ring," Al answered.

"I know it's a ring," said Fred. "But it's no ordinary one, it's an engagement ring. I'm going to ask Teresa to go steady . . . get engaged! Do you understand?"

"Yes," said Al. "Congratulations."

"Now, the problem is, I haven't told her about you; not yet, anyway. So I was wondering if you wouldn't mind keeping out of sight until I get around to telling her."

"Oh, right. I understand," said Al.

"What do you want in the Chinese?"

"I'll have king prawns and fried rice, please. Oh, and prawn crackers."

Fred put the television in the bedroom so Al could watch it. He gave his flat a good cleaning and tidy-up and had everything looking splendid. He carefully left a few books around to show he was a bit of a reader. The truth was, he never ever completed a book.

Al was interested in books but Fred had never taught him to read. Music, the cinema, and now TV was surely enough for anyone, especially a snake.

At 7.30 the doorbell rang. Fred checked his watch. He had asked Teresa to come for eight o'clock and he knew no Dublin girl arrived early for a date.

"Get the door," Fred shouted to Al. Al slithered over to the front door. "No, on second thought, I'll get it." Fred opened the door.

There stood a Chinese man. "Chop suey for two, fried rice. King prawn with fried rice." Then the Chinese man noticed Al. "Oh, very nice. How much for eel? I give you very good price."

"It's not an eel, it's a snake," said Fred.

"How much for snake? I give you very good price."

"The snake's not for sale," said Al.

10

"That's right," said Fred. He paid for the food and closed the door. "I could have made a few bob there," said Fred with a grin.

"Ah, you wouldn't sell me, would you?" asked a worried Al.

"No," said Fred warmly, "but you'd better stay in the bedroom tonight and keep the noise down."

Eight o'clock came and went. Fred looked anxious as the clock chimed eight-thirty.

Al put his head around the bedroom door. "No sign of Teresa? I hope she hasn't stood you up."

"No, she hasn't," snapped Fred. "I mean, she won't!"

"Listen Fred, I'm starving. Is there any chance I could have my food, since I'm not dining with you two lovebirds?"

Fred took out the food. "There's a great

movie starting soon, with John Wayne, called *Rio Bravo*. And you just missed a deadly episode of *Have Gun Will Travel,*" Al teased.

"Blast," said Fred. "I wish they'd invent a way of recording things off telly."

"They might, some day," said Al.

There was a loud ring. "Shush," said Fred. "That's her!"

Al kept the sound on the TV down low. He could hear lots of laughter and giggling. Then he could hear Teresa exclaiming, "Oh, it's beautiful. You're so romantic! Wait till I show the girls at work."

After a time, Al got the urge to visit the bathroom. He slid off the bed and quietly opened the bedroom door. He could see the back of Fred's Brylcreemed head and Teresa on the sofa as he sneaked by to the bathroom.

"Excuse me, darling," said Teresa. "I need to powder my nose." As she stepped into the bathroom, Fred heard an unholy scream. Teresa came rushing out of the bathroom. "There's the biggest worm I've ever seen in my life in your bathroom!"

13

Fred stuck his head into the bathroom and gave Al a dirty look. "It's only my pet snake." Fred smiled nervously. "He wouldn't hurt a fly."

"It gives me the creeps," said Teresa. "I'm not staying in a room with that!" She pointed at Al, who was trying to make his way back to the bedroom.

"It's not as if he were a cobra," Fred pleaded.

"It's a horrible slithering thing," she snapped. "It's him or me. I'm certainly not marrying anyone with a snake for a pet, it's unnatural. Why can't you have a dog or a cat like any normal person?"

Well, Fred realised it was either Al or Teresa, and since he was planning to marry Teresa and probably move to Glasnevin where Teresa's family were from, Fred knew he and Al would have to part.

One evening, not long after that, Fred brought Al down to the Tolka river. "Sorry about this, Al, but you know how it is . . .

14

besides, you're as much at home in water
as on land, more so, in fact. So, I guess it's
goodbye," he said sadly.

Al's eyes misted up. "Thanks for
everything, Fred. And for introducing me to
rock 'n' roll."

"I'll miss you too," said Fred. There was a
tremble in his voice. "You can pass yourself
off as an eel in the river. Nobody will bother
you." Al give him a big squeeze and winded
him. "Take care," said Fred, as he watched
him slip into the water and snake away.

Al lived for a few weeks in the river. He wasn't used to being in cold water all the time, so he constantly had a head cold. And he never managed to pass himself off as an eel, at least not to other eels. They thought he was a freak, which was a little upsetting for him as all he had ever known before was kindness.

Still, he made pals with a kingfisher and a dipper. They told him all about the rivers, streams and canals. There was a great variety of life there which most people hadn't noticed.

Al used to venture at night from the river to the streams, then over to the Royal Canal. Sometimes he even ventured as far as the Liffey. He became very fond of the Liffey, and stayed there for several weeks. He would swim from the Ha'penny Bridge all the way to Celbridge in County Kildare, turning at Vanessa's Bridge and then heading back to Dublin.

One of the games he played to amuse himself was to suddenly appear to anglers as they fished the river. It always startled them. Other times he would slip out of the water and climb a tree, then he would hang down on some angler and lift off his hat. This would really freak them out and when they'd look up into the willow tree they could never see him; his camouflage was too good.

One evening he was back on the banks of the Tolka having a little snakenap, when three boys happened upon him and picked him up. One grabbed his head, another his tail, and they played tug-of-war with him.

"Do you mind!" said Al. "I'm not made of rubber."

"You talk!" said one.

The others just let their jaws drop.

"Of course I do," Al retorted.

"Do you live here?" asked one of the boys.

"Here and there," said Al. "I live the life of a rover."

"That's cool," said one boy.

"Oh, the water can be very cool at times." Al's body shivered as if to prove the point.

"Do you want to come home for tea?" asked another boy.

"Well, that's very nice," said Al. "I haven't had a cup of tea for weeks and I really miss it."

"I'm Tommy. This is Willie and that's Tony."

Then the snake introduced himself. "I'm Al. I used to live in Homefarm Road. But now I've no permanent abode."

"You can stay in our place. I know my ma and da wouldn't mind. My da has tropical fish so you'll be at home there."

"What do you mean?" Al wondered.

"Well, you're an anaconda from South America, the Amazon river or somewhere like that."

"You really think I'm an anaconda? asked Al. "But they're huge!"

"Well, they start small," said Tony.

Al looked down at his body with a puzzled expression.

"Let's go," said Tommy.

"Wait a minute," said Al. "I have an idea." He made a circle with his body then, with his head, grabbed hold of his tail. "Would one of you mind pushing me along? It will help me get there faster."

Tommy pushed him like a hoop down the road. "This is great fun," said Tommy.

"Can I try?" said Willie.

Things were going fine until they came to a hill. Suddenly, Al began to pick up speed. He went rolling down the hill at a great pace. The boys raced after him, trying to keep up. Out he went on to the road, passing cars and buses. A man on a bicycle was so surprised to see the snake racing by that he fell off the bike.

Then a policeman stepped off the footpath to stop the object, which he thought was a bicycle tyre. Al couldn't stop himself. He knocked the policeman down and rolled over him. Realising what had gone over him, the policeman picked himself up and ran down the road in the opposite direction.

Al rolled into a shop, bounced off the wall and ended on a pile of leather shoes that were on display. He let go his tail. The sales assistant, who hadn't seen Al roll in, went over to the lady who was buying shoes.

"What about these?" He picked up Al and a lady's shoe. "These are genuine snakeskin." The lady looked at the snake, screamed then fainted.

When the assistant realised what he was holding in his left hand was a real snake, he too fainted. Al, realising that the shoes were snakeskin, also fainted.

When he woke up, he was in a warm house beside a cosy fireplace. Three smiling faces looked down at him.

"Are you all right?" said the woman. "Tommy tells me you were abandoned. That's terrible!" Tommy's mother sighed. "Well, don't you worry, we'll make sure you have a proper roof over your head and a decent meal in your stomach."

Al had really landed on his feet, so to speak. Things couldn't have been better in the O'Connell household. Four meals a day and lots of company. Tommy's dad was delighted to discover Al had a keen interest in music. He introduced Al to the sound of the big brass bands and to opera singers like Mario Lanza, Maria Callas, Gigli, Caruso, Bjorling. It wasn't Elvis, but Al got to like opera a lot.

Mrs O'Connell found Al a great help around the house. He was good at things like dusting and he could get into those tricky corners of the room that she couldn't reach.

Tommy used to regularly bring Al down to the park. There he enjoyed playing games. Sometimes he would be a spear in the game if they were playing Robin Hood and his Merry Men. If it was Cowboys and Indians, Al usually ended up as a rope when one of the cowboys was captured by the Indians. Occasionally he would make a loop around a branch and they'd pretend to hang somebody. Sometimes, Al made his body into a swing and hung from a heavy branch. The smaller children would sit in him, he was lovely and soft. Al would gently swing himself back and forwards.

When the boys went to school, Al would sometimes go with Tommy's dad on his bike. He was a window cleaner. Al was very helpful and could put a wonderful shine on the glass, buffing it with his body, so much so that Tommy's dad got more work because of Al.

In the evening Al would sit on a couch and watch Tommy reading his comics, and Mrs O'Connell reading her magazines, and Mr O'Connell his evening newspapers, and he'd feel a little envious. Tommy's mother began to realise the need Al had to read. So she arranged with Mr Weir, her first cousin and the principal of the national school, for Al to attend. Mainly to learn to read and write.

Al was very excited about the whole idea. But, when he went to the school, he was a bit disappointed that he was not in the classroom with Tommy, Willie and Tony. Instead, he was put into Senior Infants with Miss Hall as his teacher. She was very pretty and she had a wonderful voice. Al sat with the other boys and girls, and had great fun painting and sticking things together.

When Miss Hall was teaching the alphabet, Al suddenly got a brain-wave. "Teacher! Teacher!"

"What is it, Al?"

Her voice was so sweet Al felt like blushing – and that was very unusual for a snake. "I was wondering if I could help by making the shapes of the letters."

She moved closer and blinked her beautiful doe-like eyes. "Do you think you could manage all those tricky shapes?"

"I'll try," said Al, all coy.

"Right, children, pay attention. We're going to ask Al to perform the alphabet.

We'll start with the letter A for Apple." Al quickly looked at the picture of the A on the wall and twisted his shape into an A. "Well done, Al, that's very clever." Then he even made the shape of an apple!

When Mr Weir, the principal, found out how well the children had learned the alphabet he was very pleased.

Al learned so quickly that Mr Weir decided to move him up several grades until he was in the same class as his pals. In geography he learned all about South America, the tropical rainforests and the Amazon river. His heart gave a little flutter every time someone mentioned the Amazon river, he didn't know why.

After school, when the boys had a football match, Al would get a chance to be the goalpost for Tommy's team while the other side had to use their sweaters as markers.

Of course, it wasn't always easy in

school. The school bully picked on him several times and called him a snake in the grass or a black-hearted viper. Al found it a bit upsetting. Tommy decided to take on the school bully who was bigger and tougher than he was.

They met after school alongside the river and they were going to have it out, as they say. Al hated violence in real life; he didn't mind it on television or films for Fred the Ted told him it wasn't real, only pretend. Al didn't want his pal Tommy getting a black eye or a bleeding nose on account of him. So, when all their schoolmates gathered around to witness the fight between Tommy and the school bully, Al wriggled into the centre to stop the fight. The bully told Al to get out of the way, that he was only a yellow-belly. "An overgrown worm!"

Al was a patient snake but his patience was not inexhaustible. "Right," he declared to Tommy. "He's picked on me so I'll fight him."

The bully laughed loudly. "I'd like to see you try to give me a box in the snot" (which, as you know, means a punch in the nose). The bully's friends laughed loudly. Then the bully took a swipe and punched Al in the face. He crashed down on the grassy bank and began to see stars.

Willie hurried down to the river and cupped some water in his hands, then splashed it over Al's face. "Are you all right?" he asked anxiously.

Al wriggled, then sat up. "Fine!"

"We are the champions," yelled the bully and his friends.

"Not so fast," Al said. He knew he couldn't let his friends down. He remembered what John Wayne would do in a situation like this. The bully took another swipe at Al. He quickly drew his body back and the bully fell flat on his face. Everyone laughed. The bully was really mad and tried to kick Al. Al's tail was too quick for him. He gripped the bully by the leg, lifted him into the air then dropped him in the river. The bully dragged himself out of the water. He was soaking wet and very muddy. And very impressed.

"Fancy some more of the same?" said Al. "Or would you like to wake up with a crowd around you?"

"I give up," said the bully. "You win." He went home dripping wet.

"Hope he doesn't catch a chill," said Al, feeling guilty.

"He won't be bothering anyone else in school again," said Tommy.

"You're a hero," said Willie and Tony. They all cheered and carried Al home.

"Let's go for fish and chips," said Al.

"None of us has any money," said the others.

"I have an idea," said Al. "Follow me."

The group went into the village. "Anybody got a hat?" Al asked as they put him on the pavement. One boy produced a woolly hat. Al placed it up-side-down on the ground near him and began to perform the alphabet for passers-by.

"What's your name, sir?"

"Freddy," said the man. Al immediately made the shape of an F. "That's very clever," said the man, and threw him a sixpenny coin. Al winked at the others who were standing nearby.

Another man walked down the street in pink trousers, a blue jacket, a cravat, and wearing a beret. "How amusing! A busking snake. Can you make the letter Q for Quentin?"

"I'll have a go." It proved rather difficult but he made a good attempt.

"How splendid," said the man and threw him a half-crown coin.

Then a voice from behind asked, "Can you do the letter G?"

"Yes," said Al, as he looked round. There was the policeman he had rolled over a few months ago. Al stammered the word, "Gu . . . gu . . . G?"

"Yes," said the policeman. "G . . . for gaol!"

Well, you have never seen a snake move so fast down the road, with his friends running behind him, and the policeman yellhollering, "Come back here!"

When they finally got away from the policeman, they stopped to get their breath back. "Oh, no," said Al. "I left the money behind."

"Yes, but I didn't," laughed Tony.

They all laughed loudly and headed down to the local chipper. Al had made enough money to buy fish and chips for all. As they left the takeaway, two men watched from the shadows of an alley.

"There he goes," said one of the men. They got into their van and slowly followed Al and his pals down the road, keeping close to the kerb. As they approached Al and the boys, one man jumped out of the back of the van carrying a sack. Before Al realised what was happening, a sack was put over his head and he was bundled into it.

Tommy, Tony and Willie tried to stop it happening but the man was too strong and too fast. As quick as a flash, the sack was thrown into the back of the van. The man jumped in and the driver sped away.

The boys ran down the road, shouting: "Stop, thieves! They've kidnapped Al!"

But there was just one elderly man standing in his garden. When he wondered what all the fuss was about, they asked could they use his telephone, as their friend Al had just been kidnapped. The man was shocked and invited them in. But, when they told him Al was an anaconda from Drumcondra, he showed them the door.

As the door slammed behind them, Willie said, "I don't think he believed us."

Al found himself on a ship; he recognised the sounds from television programmes. Luckily he didn't suffer from seasickness, for he was very hot and cramped in the sack. He was glad he'd had the fish and chips as he hadn't been fed since his capture, and he knew that was at least two days ago.

He was carried off the ship and hidden in a big suitcase under smelly clothes. Then he was put on a train. He'd have loved to look out the window and see where he was going. The train journey seemed longer than the ship. He heard the suitcase being opened then the sack being untied. A rough-looking man with a mean grin peered in.

"He's still OK, Sid."

"Good. Hey, Jimmy, you'd better feed him."

Al felt a piece of bread land on his head. It was toast with marmalade. He quickly swallowed it. He could have eaten several sliced pans but the sack was resealed immediately. After the train journey he was put in a taxi.

"I hope this pet shop is open and that he has our loot."

"Relax," said Sid. "Everything will be fine. People will pay a good price for a talking snake."

"Only, let me do the dealing."

"Sure, Jimmy. You have a flair for that sort of thing."

Al could hear the roar of the traffic. He knew he was in a big city.

"Here's the place," said Sid to the taxi-driver.

"*Reggie's Exotic Pet Shop.* Its slogan: Whatever You Want We Can Get! Nothing too big or small."

"That's the place all right," smiled Sid.

"Good morning, gents, I'm Reggie," they were greeted as they entered the pet shop. "And what can I do you for?" he sniggered. "Can I interest you in a nice canary, or perhaps a macaw? Expensive, but makes a great pet. What about a tarantula?"

"No, we're the ones who phoned you from Dublin. I'm Sid, this is Jimmy."

"Pleased to meet you boys," said Reggie. Then, noticing the suitcase Jimmy was carrying, he rubbed his hands. "Give us a look." The lid was slowly lifted and the sack undone. At last Al could see some light. Then a big hand grabbed him by the neck and pulled him out of the sack. "It's a bit small and scrawny . . . I thought it would be much fatter and bigger."

"It's still growing," said Jimmy. "After a couple of good feeds, it will fill out."

Reggie picked up Al and put him over his shoulders. "What do you think?" He began to dance around the pet shop. "Tanya the exotic dancer!" They all grinned broadly. The macaw and the parrot started making a racket. "Quiet!" yelled Reggie. "You see, boys, there's this dancer called Tanya who lost one of her pythons and she asked me to look out for a replacement. If I can pass ole Al here off as a python I'm laughing, if you get my meaning." Then he scratched his head. "You did say it talks?"

"Yes," said Jimmy. "It's educated."

"OK, Al. Let's hear you." Al sat silent. He refused to speak.

"Go on, you squirmy worm, speak!" said Jimmy, prodding him with his index finger.

"I'll have you know I'm no worm. The last time . . . oops." Al realised he was talking.

"That's pretty good," said Reggie. "Nearly as good as Judy, my macaw."

38

"Don't compare me with no reptile," snapped the bird.

"Quiet!" growled Reggie.

"Well, boys, you've got me a real find there." He placed Al inside a large plate-glass case and put the lid on. "Well, I suppose we'd better get down to brass tacks and talk lolly. Now, boys, you know times are hard in this business. It's getting very difficult to make a crust with all the overheads and feeding all the stock I carry. Say, two hundred," said Reggie.

"Are you joking me? said Jimmy. "Two hundred for a talking snake! Five hundred."

"Listen, boys, there's a drop in the market. Too many of these 'Save the Planet' types taking over. There isn't the interest in this type of item. Ten years ago I was selling alligators, now I can't get one. Three hundred and I write you a chicken's neck – cheque."

"Three hundred and we'll take cash," said Jimmy.

Reggie laughed. "You're my type of businessman."

They spat on their palms then shook hands. Reggie handed over the money and they left. "Call me if you find anything else interesting," he shouted after them. Then the owner peered at Al. "You are going to make me a lot of money." His expression changed and became very sinister. "You'd better talk and do the business for me, otherwise I'll sell you to a leather factory and I'll *still* make money. Do you receive my meaning?"

Al felt a cold sweat breaking out over all his body. He nodded. "I mean . . . yes, I understand, Reggie."

"Good," said the owner.

Lying in the glass case reminded Al of the great times he'd had with Fred the Ted in Drumcondra. Then he began to think of the

O'Connells, Tommy and his friends Willie and Tony. He missed them dearly. When the pet shop closed and Reggie had gone home, Al asked Judy the macaw where they were.

"You may be able to speak," she snapped, "but you're not very bright, are you? We're in London, silly."

London! Al had always wanted to visit London; not this way, of course. He'd love to visit all the great places in London he'd seen on TV. Even the red buses would be a treat to see. But now he wondered if he would ever see outside this shop. What he'd really fancy at this very moment in time was to sit on a soft sofa with some fish and chips and watch a good Western film, but it wasn't to be.

Al felt rather lonely in the pet shop, despite the number of creatures there. The macaw refused to speak to him. In the tanks either side of him were piranha fish. All they did was flash their teeth and look at him as if they wished he was their next meal. The little birds were a bit freaked by him. Still, in the mornings Al loved to hear their sweet song. The spider monkey, who on occasion was let out of his cage, would hurry over to Al, give the glass a hard thump, then run away making all kinds of monkey faces. Al tried to ignore him but it wasn't always easy.

One morning, as soon as Reggie opened the shop, a long black car pulled up outside. The car door opened and out stepped a lady with two men, one on either side of her. The door of the shop swung open and Tanya the dancer swept in, her long leopard-skin coat brushing the floor as she moved.

"Where is it, Reggie? I'm just dying to see it. Oh, do show me."

"Good morning, Madam Tanya." He eyed the two men in black suits with fedora hats pulled over one eye. They grinned at him; their gold fillings flashed in their toothy smiles.

The dancer paced up and down the long narrow pet shop. "Where is the beast?" she yelled, becoming impatient and throwing her arms in the air. Like a crab, Reggie moved sideways down the shop, keeping one eye on the dancer and the other on the two tough bodyguards.

"There it is, hiding behind this log." He banged the glass hard. Al's head popped up.

"I hope it won't suffer from stage fright," Tanya snapped.

"No, no," said Reggie. "This slippery chap is used to people. Loves children, especially for dessert." Reggie laughed and winked. He could see that Tanya wasn't amused.

"I am an *artiste*," she declared, as if she was addressing a large audience. "I only work with professionals."

"Oh, this snake is a pro." Reggie tried to

take him out of the glass case, but Al was holding on to the log for dear life. Reggie grinned, a little embarrassed. Then he prodded Al with his pen. Al hissed as he let go. "Did you ever see such a beautiful specimen?" asked Reggie. He stroked Al.

"Doesn't look like my last royal python."

"No? Well, it's a rarer variety. Cleopatra owned one similar to this."

"I thought she had an asp," said Judy the macaw.

"You shut your beak," yelled Reggie. "Fancy a parrot trying to give me a history lesson."

The dancer poked Al several times along the body. "Here, give him to me." She whipped the snake from the owner and placed it over her shoulder. "He's quite heavy," she complained. Then she moved her hands up and down his body.

Al began to laugh uncontrollably. "Oh, hee, hee . . . stop, ha ha . . . that tickles . . ."

"It does talk," said Tanya. A broad smile broke over her red lips. "I'll take it, darling Reggie!"

"Wise decision. Very hard to come by, these anacondas, I mean, pythons."

"I hope it gets on well with Jezebel, my Indian python. She's very jealous of me showing affection to anyone else."

"Oh, they'll get on like a house on fire. Don't you worry. Now, I hate to talk filthy lucre to a star like yourself . . ."

"How much? said Tanya, her pen and cheque book in hand.

"Well, it's normally twelve hundred pounds for such a rare specimen, but for you, a thousand. And at that it's a steal," he grinned, rubbing his hands as the cheque was being signed. "No need to wrap it, I'm sure."

Tanya left in a flurry with Al still around her neck.

Reggie danced around the shop and kissed the cheque, then hugged the macaw who squawked loudly and flew around the room.

Al found himself in a big apartment in Fulham. Tanya introduced him to Jezebel. The Indian python slipped out of her wicker basket and over to him.

"You two darlings get acquainted. I'm going to have a bath and relax before tonight's show."

The python blinked her green eyes at Al and gently coiled her body around his. Al smiled broadly. Her tail reached up around his neck. Then she squeezed tightly. "Listen, buster. I'm the star of this show and you'd better remember it. The last act will be with Tanya and me, so you don't take a curtain call." She squeezed tighter. "Is that understood?"

"Yes," said Al, gasping for breath and nodding his head frantically.

"Good!" She disentangled herself, then added, "Just so we understand each other."

Al was feeling very nervous about the performance in the Coconut Club in Soho. He enjoyed the stage and remembered the time he'd been in the school play with his friends Tommy, Tony, Willie and the other pupils. He'd played *all*

the serpents in a play about St Patrick. The audience loved him and he got three curtain calls. He felt sad just thinking about it.

Tanya kissed the two snakes. "Are you ready, my darlings?" she asked. Al thought she looked very pretty, with her long black hair falling over her shoulders and her sequined dress.

"You look lovely," said Al.

"Why, thank you," said Tanya. "That's so sweet of you."

Jezebel bit him on the tail. He shrieked. "Shush," said the stage-manager. "You're on as soon as Eddie Docker is finished."

Al watched the comedian standing in the spotlight. He was wearing a grey suit with big black spots on it. The audience seemed to be really enjoying themselves. Al found that listening to the jokes made him relax and feel less nervous.

"In the jungle, these cannibals captured a comedian. They began to eat him. Then one says to the other: 'Does this taste funny?'"

The audience were bursting their sides laughing, so was Al. He hung around the stage-manager, with tears coming out of his eyes.

"That fella kills me," said Al.

"Pull yourself together," said the stage-manager.

The comedian continued. "I met my wife in the tunnel of love . . . she was digging it. My wife's teeth are like stars . . . they come out at night."

Al started laughing again. "Did you hear that? Hee, hee!"

"Yes," said Tanya. "Several times. Be still."

Al's laughter was echoing backstage, indeed his whole body was shaking with laughter.

Jezebel picked up a jug of water and poured it over Al's head. "That might cool you off," she hissed.

"Well, you've been a great audience," said the comedian. "But, before I go, I must tell you about a boxer I knew. He was called Rembrandt, spent most of his time on the canvas! Goodnight. If you enjoyed the show, tell your friends. If you didn't, send your enemies along."

"Well done, Eddie," said Tanya. "You were great."

"Break a leg," said Eddie.

Jungle music played on the bongos as Tanya danced on to the stage with the two snakes wrapped around her. Al was still laughing from the jokes.

"Quiet," the dancer whispered from the side of her mouth, at the same time trying to keep smiling at the audience. Every time she touched any part of Al's body, he laughed. It got louder and louder. The audience began to laugh. Soon they were all laughing with Al.

"They're getting more laughs than the comedian," said the owner.

Tanya was furious. She twirled and twirled around and around, holding the two snakes high above her head. Al began to feel very dizzy. In the next part, where the two snakes were to make a heart shape and the dancer was to limbo dance through them, Al tried to stay stiff but his head was spinning; and when he touched off Jezebel's head he just collapsed on her, bringing the python and the dancer crashing down on to the stage floor. The audience laughed and cheered.

Tanya stormed off the stage, dragging the two snakes by their tails behind her. Al was then locked in the python's wicker basket. Jezebel was furious, as she wanted to curl up in her basket instead of lying around in the room when Tanya was in one of her moods.

Al could hear the voices in the next room.

"I've never been so humiliated in all my life," she yelled. "I could strangle that snake . . . and Reggie, for selling it to me!"

"I think we can arrange some cement shoes for that snake," sniggered one bodyguard. "If you know what I mean."

"No, let's sell him to the leather factory. You'll double your money."

"I don't care what happens to it, but I want to be rid of it. It ruined my performance and upset dear Jezebel."

"It will be done tonight," said one of the men.

Al trembled in the basket. He peered out through the slits and saw that Jezebel was dozing. "Jezebel, Jezebel," hissed Al.

She opened one eye. "I've nothing to say to you. First you ruin the act, then you end up in my basket."

"You are a fine performer, the best I've ever seen . . ." (Al had never seen a snake dancer before, but he was living on his wits and knew that he had to escape those two bodyguards.) "I'm prepared to leave the show and never return."

The python's eyes widened and she sidled up to the basket. "Do you really mean it?"

"Yes," said Al. "I realise I've no talent. I'm not cut out for show business."

"Well, I could have told you that before, but we were prepared to give you the chance even if you blew it. People think performing comes easily, but you've got to feel it in every inch of your body . . ."

"Yes," said Al. "That's what you do. You are the Sarah Bernhardt of the reptile world."

The python looked puzzled (she didn't know who Sarah Bernhardt was and decided to take it as a compliment) but seemed very pleased. Al wondered how he could convince her to open the catch on the basket without her becoming suspicious.

"Yes," said Al. "I'll leave tomorrow after I get a good sleep in this most comfortable bed. Aaah, it's so cosy." Al gave a mock yawn.

Jezebel flicked the catch open with her tongue. "Out! Now!"

"But . . ." said Al.

"No buts, out and don't come back." Al slipped out as the python slipped in. Then Al heard footsteps and the door opening. He hid down beside the couch.

Two men sneaked over to the basket, picked it up and carried it out. "Fancy a pair of snakeskin shoes, Joey?" said the other bodyguard. They laughed loudly as they carried the python away.

Al snaked out the window, shimmied down the drainpipe and slithered out into the cold, wet streets. He began to feel guilty about what might happen to Jezebel, so he hurried into a phone box and placed a reverse-charge call, explaining to the

55

operator that he hadn't any coins and must get an urgent message to Tanya the dancer. Tanya agreed to accept the call. Al tried to disguise his voice and explained how he

got a tip-off that her lovely python was heading for the leather factory. She shrieked, then thanked him for the call, offering him free tickets for her show on Friday night at the Coconut Club. He felt better after that.

Then he began to get hunger pangs. He wandered around for a long time, checking the bins for any scraps of food. Then he saw two men walking down the road. He climbed into a tree. "Yes, it's a grand place," said one. "Not far from Charing Cross station. I've lived there over two years now. No one bothers you. You can choose any room in the block. It's one of the best squats around and very few people know about it. It's rent free," he sniggered. "Couldn't ask for better."

Al was listening, so intently that he lost his grip on the branch and came crashing down on the two young men. They got such a fright they ran like hares down the road. Al followed after them, but kept a safe distance for fear they might be hostile to him for frightening them.

He saw them later leaving a Chinese

takeaway and called after them. Once they got over the initial shock of a snake, *and* a talking one, they began to relax and offered him some spring roll and sweet-and-sour pork. Al explained his situation to them. They felt very sorry for him and invited him to stay with them.

Al was delighted with the company and settled very nicely into his new home. He lived in one of the top rooms of the block. There he had a splendid view of London. Gerry and Michael, his new friends, were

buskers. They both played guitar and sang, mainly Beatles songs. Al soon became a big fan of the Beatles and all the other groups that were popular at the time – The

Rolling Stones, Gerry and the Pacemakers,
Freddy and the Dreamers, Cliff Richard and
the Shadows.

When his pals were off gigging around the
London streets, Al would laze on top of the
roof and watch the people go by in the red
buses and the London cabs. Sometimes he
got a strange feeling, like a longing for
something, but he did not know what. He
really wanted to go out and wander around
the city. Dogs, cats could do it, even birds,

especially pigeons – they wandered about to their hearts' content. Yet he knew he couldn't slide and crawl about the place.

So Al began to practise shaping the lower part of his body to be like legs. He got himself an old raincoat and a cap, and he decided to head out and explore this exciting city. He had read as much as he could about the city from books lying around in the flat, so when he arrived at a  tourist spot he knew exactly where he was. Piccadilly Circus was the first stop in his exploration of the city. Then he wandered down Regent Street. It was so exciting looking at the many shops. He was a bit nervous, with all the crowds, but no one took any notice of him.

As he passed along St James's Park, he came to Buckingham Palace. There was a group of tourists standing by the gate listening to a guide. Al peered through the bars, hoping to see the queen, but all he saw was a soldier glaring back at him.

"The palace was built by George the Third for twenty-one thousand pounds," said the guide.

"Sorry, that's wrong," said Al. "It was built for the Duke of Buckingham in the 18th century. It was he who sold it to George the Third for twenty-one thousand pounds."

The guide wasn't too pleased at being corrected, but ignored him. "Over there," he continued, "is a mulberry garden planted by Queen Victoria . . ."

"Excuse me for interrupting," said Al. "But it was planted by James the First. He wanted to encourage the making of silk in England."

The guide came down to Al with a big smile on his face. "Listen, mate. You seem to be a bit of a walking encyclopaedia. How about working for me? I'd pay you a fiver a day. I'm just standing in for the real guide who's down with the flu."

Al was delighted to be asked, and agreed to be a stand-in guide. It was a great way to visit all the historic places and get paid for it.

Things went fine for months. Al read every book he could about London and the

historical sites, and soon he was an official

guide. He became popular with all the tourists. Whether they were Japanese, American or Russian, Al seemed to be able to communicate with them all.

Before long he was something of a celebrity around London. Whether it was in Poet's Corner, Westminster Abbey, St Paul's Cathedral, Madame Tussaud's, The Tate Gallery or Regent's Park, Al was able to regale his clients with its history and some interesting stories. He could quote Shakespeare, Bacon, or Keats at the drop of a coin into his cap.

Life was good for Al. He would treat his new friends to shows in the West End and go to fancy restaurants. But he never forgot his old pals back home in Dublin, sending them presents for their birthdays and gifts for his old school.

One evening, life took a turn for the worse for Al. It all began when he got the urge to have a swim in the London Lido.

He was spotted by the manager of the Lido, who phoned the London Zoo. Next minute, Al was nabbed by two big strong RSPCA men and stuffed into a sack. Not again, he thought. He didn't fancy ending up in another pet shop. When he was removed from the sack, he was dropped into a small pool in a large glass-fronted cage.

"Where am I?" Al asked a lizard in the next cage.

"You're in the zoo, mate. And a lifer, I reckon."

Al, who was used to the freedom of the city, couldn't bear to be cooped up again. He began to feel very depressed. Then he heard strange laughter that seemed to echo all round the zoo.

"What's he so happy about?" Al enquired.

"That's a spotted hyena," said the chameleon. "He sees the funny side of everything, especially you getting nicked."

"I'd love to give him a piece of my mind," Al grumbled.

Al curled up like a rope and tried to sleep. But, as soon as it got dark, there was a cacophony of sounds. Lions roaring, leopards growling, monkeys shrieking, owls hooting and the hyena laughing his head off. Al was used to drifting off to sleep to the pleasant tones of Simon and Garfunkel or Bob Dylan. How could anyone sleep with this racket? Next morning, Al awoke bleary-eyed. He had only managed to snatch a little sleep during the night.

"Rise and shine," said a voice from the

other cage. "It's important we look smart for my subjects."

Al looked up to discover a large snake with a hood which was raised. It was holding itself very stiffly. "What's he going on about?" Al asked the lizard.

"That's a king-cobra from India. He thinks all the visitors who come into the reptile house are subjects who've come to pay homage to him."

"What visitors?" Al wondered.

Just then, the doors swung open and a school tour arrived into the reptile house. The young boys rushed around the room banging on the heavy glass, and pressing their faces up to the glass making the ugliest faces they could manage.

"Look at that big fat one there," said one boy, pointing to Al. "Move!" the boy yelled. "You're like a dead log."

Al ignored them.

"Hey! look at this one," said another as

they watched the king-cobra sway from side to side. One boy pulled a large wad of bubble-gum out of his mouth and spread it on the glass. The cobra was furious and coiled itself behind a log.

"Let's go, this is boring," said another boy. "I know. We'll go and tease the monkeys in the monkey house."

"Did you ever see anything like it?" hissed the cobra.

The crocodile emerged from his narrow pool. "You think chewing-gum is bad? They drop pennies on me all the time. It's most annoying."

"Listen," said Al.

"To what?" the lizard wondered.

"It's the *Animals*."

"So what?" said the chameleon.

"No, the group, I mean . . . *There is a house in New Orleans . . .*" Al began to sing.

"You're weird," said the iguana.

"Great song," said Al. "Where's the music coming from?"

"Probably Kenny, the keeper. He carries a transistor around with him all the time."

Kenny entered the reptile house with a brush and a bin to take up all the sweet wrappers and crisp bags.

"Paint It Black," said Al, as he listened to the radio. "I love the Rolling Stones."

Kenny turned around quickly but could see no one. He scratched his head. He was sure he'd heard a voice saying the name of the song on his radio.

"Oh, turn that up. *Are You Lonesome Tonight*! I haven't heard Elvis for ages." Kenny looked all around but couldn't see any visitor. He picked up the radio and put his ear to it. "Is that Radio Caroline?" Al asked.

Kenny shrieked and ran out of the reptile house. "That's a pity," said Al. "I was really enjoying the music. It was cheering me up no end."

Next minute the door opened and four keepers crept in carrying brooms, brushes and poles.

"I'm telling you, this place is haunted!" said Kenny. "I could hear voices and nobody but me was here. And they weren't in my head!" he added.

"Maybe it was one of those reptiles," said another zoo-keeper, laughing loudly.

"That's correct," said Al.

"Who said that?" Kenny trembled.

"Over here, guys," said Al. The keepers all turned around. There was Al, swinging to the sound of the music. "Cool! Hey!" said Al.

All the keepers fainted. When they came round, Al was pressed up to the glass. "Listen lads, I'm sorry . . . I didn't mean to startle you. It's just I love music, especially good ole rock 'n' roll."

The keepers stood there wide-eyed. "You really can talk?"

"Sure," said Al. "'To be or not to be, that is the question'. Shakespeare. Or how about 'Get off that horse!' John Wayne!" Al chuckled.

"Blimey," said Kenny. "Not only is he a music fan, but a film buff as well."

"And he can quote Shakespeare," said another.

Al was removed from his glass case and brought to the keepers' room. There he regaled them with stories and talked to them about his favourite films and TV shows. The zoo-keepers were as delighted with Al's company as he was with theirs.

After the zoo closed for the evening, the keepers stayed on and had something to eat in the canteen. "What would you like, Al?" Kenny enquired. "A piece of raw meat?"

"No thanks, Kenny. I'd fancy a batter burger and chips."

"You all right?" said Kenny as he helped Al to some tomato sauce for his chips.

Al was not returned to the reptile house. Instead, he slept in a wooden crate with plenty of warm straw. The keepers were very proud of Al and would bring him on tours around the zoo early morning or late afternoon, when the curator wasn't around. They all felt Mr Simpson wouldn't approve of having an anaconda as a pet on the premises.

Al got to know all the animals – the elephants and cheetahs, the hippopotamus, zebras, camels, and so many more. He couldn't get over the variety of creatures in the zoo.

He even got to like the hyena. Al would tell him some old jokes he'd heard from Fred the Ted back in Drumcondra and Eddie Docker from the Coconut Club. The hyena would roll around laughing in his cage.

Al was getting used to zoo life. He was being well fed and had a roof over his head. He had good friends, yet there was still an emptiness inside he couldn't explain. He put it down to hunger but he knew it wasn't that. Well, if he had to spend his life in the zoo so be it, he thought. Surrounded with wildfolk and friendly humans.

Al wasn't to know that things were about to change dramatically for him once again. The curator had ordered the old crates to be removed from the storage house, as a new assignment of wildlife was arriving, including a giant panda from China.

Al was awakened from a deep sleep by the sound of voices.

"Only one more crate, Bert, and that's it. We'll go straight to the city dump, drop this lot and have breakfast in Oxford Street," Bruce retorted.

"Why wait until Oxford Street?" asked Bert.

"Because that's where we have to collect the old office furniture."

"Oh yeah, I forgot about that," said Bert. "I know where we can sell the lot, and we'll make fifty quid each before lunchtime."

"Sell these crates?" wondered Bert.

"No, the furniture," growled Bruce. "Come on, let's load this crate."

Al bumped his head when the crate was moved. "Ouch!" he yelled.

"Did you hear that?" said Bruce. "I think it came from inside the crate."

"Don't be ridiculous," said Bert. "They're hardly going to leave something asleep in a crate."

"Well, it could be an animal or something, hiding," insisted Bruce.

"Is that so?" snapped Bert. "Let's go. I want to beat the rush-hour traffic."

They loaded the last crate and headed out

of the zoo as the keepers were arriving in. Kenny and the other zoo-keepers were shocked to discover the crate with Al in it was gone. They could only hope he would be all right and find his way back to wherever he came from.

"Did you get the money from that zoo fellow?" asked Bruce.

"Yes," said Bert. "And do you know what he said we should do with the crates? . . . recycle them."

"Isn't that ridiculous," said Bruce. "Blimey it's only timber, there's lots more where that came from . . . "

Al wanted to argue with them about the merits of recycling, but decided to keep silent.

After a long journey they arrived at one of the city's dumps. "Lift!" yelled Bert.

"These crates are bloomin' heavy," said Bruce. "Now, over the edge."

Al didn't like the sound of that. The next thing, he was banging from side to side then top to bottom as the crate rolled down the hill. Then the crate crashed to the ground, shattering and splintering into pieces. Al was knocked out.

When Al awoke, all he could see were stars. "Is it night already?" he wondered. Then his head began to throb and ache and he remembered what had happened. Gulls were screaming overhead and swooping down at him. "Get off," he yelled as he crawled away.

He passed over fridges, old cars, oil drums. Then he spotted a black bag with its contents spilling out. "Clothes!" Al exclaimed. He wriggled into a black polo-neck sweater and grey slacks. Then he found a fur hat, a bit moth-eaten but it was fine for Al, as the weather was getting colder. That's one thing he missed about the glass case in the zoo; it was lovely and warm.

Al hung around in the dump until it was dusk. He wasn't bothered by the gulls any more since he'd put the clothes on. He waited near the entrance where he knew a refuse truck, having offloaded its rubbish, would return to the city. Sure enough, one came along, emptied its load and turned to head back for the city, the driver not realising that he was carrying precious cargo *out* of the dump. Al sat inside the skip, relaxed and stretched out. The smell was terrible but it beat walking or slithering all the way back to London.

Al jumped out at Shaftesbury Avenue and strolled up to Piccadilly Circus, then back to his squat. When he turned the corner for home he stopped abruptly. He could not believe his eyes. The building he'd been living in had been completely demolished, nothing left but a pile of rubbish.

Al was very depressed. His friends were gone. He was tired, cold, hungry and he ached all over. He wandered back to Leicester Square. There was a lovely smell of hot dogs and roasted chestnuts in the air. His tummy rumbled, his mouth watered.

He would have loved to go to the pictures, but he was broke, so he decided to go into the square and sleep, hoping he would feel better in the morning. Most of the benches were occupied by lonely old men who had the same idea. Al decided he would sleep on one of the statues. He looked over at Charlie Chaplin. This made him smile, remembering some of the Saturday mornings in Fred's flat in Drumcondra watching old silent movies of Charlie Chaplin.

But Al's smile soon faded when a cold wind blew, so he climbed up on to the statue of Shakespeare. He looked at the bard, who had his chin in his hand.

"You, too, look like you'd rather be somewhere else." As he coiled around the head and shoulders, he spoke to the statue. "If only you were really here, Will, we would have so much to talk about. I'd love to ask you some things about *Hamlet* and *Othello,* and whether Richard Burbage was as good an actor as Laurence Olivier. Also, I'd tell you how much I love quoting from your book of sonnets, which I picked up in a second-hand bookshop in Dublin."

A pigeon landed on the statue and cooed. Taking no notice of him, Al soon went into a deep sleep despite the noise of the city.

Al awoke and stretched. All his aches were gone. He felt good but very hungry. He took a deep breath, then an idea popped into his head to make some money. It was an inspired idea. "It must be because I slept on the statue of Shakespeare. Thank you, Will," said Al, as he climbed down from the plinth and headed for the first big bookshop he could find.

There, he asked the assistant if he could have a look at any reference books on the Book of Kells. The pretty young assistant was very helpful and laid out three books showing the beautiful manuscript's pages in colour. Al spent most of the morning poring over the pages and looking at the different designs. He would have stayed longer in the lovely warm shop, but the manager began to give him hard stares, so Al left.

He headed for Covent Garden, where there were several buskers performing. One was doing circus acts on a one-wheeled cycle. Another was spitting flames out from his mouth and juggling three flaming sticks. Al wouldn't fancy trying that, but the crowd really enjoyed it and threw him lots of coins.

When they finished, Al nervously moved into position and began to perform designs from the Book of Kells. The crowd went wild and applauded Al loudly and threw lots of coins into his hat. Even the other buskers came over and clapped him on the back when he'd finished his act. They had never seen anything like it, it was so novel, so original. Al was very pleased and his spirits were raised again. He went away and had a hearty late breakfast.

For the next few days, Al performed in front of large groups in Covent Garden to wonderful applause and financial reward. He had money for food but had not managed to find a proper place to stay. He slept in different places each evening.

One night he decided to sleep on the top of

a juggernaut truck, where he was safe from people stepping on him and cats pestering him, as they were wont to do. It was a cold clear night. Al stretched and yawned and then coiled up into a comfortable position. He loved to star-gaze and, on this frosty night, the stars looked clear and beautiful. There was no reflective light from the city to hamper his view. He could pick out Polaris, the North Star, and the Plough. He even saw a shooting star, which pleased him. After a time he drifted off into a deep sleep.

He began to dream he was going on a long journey, a mystery tour. There was a strong, cold wind blowing and he found it difficult to sit up. Then he woke with a start, for he could hear the roar of traffic and feel the ground moving under him. Too late, he realised it was no dream. He was on a big motorway on top of this truck, racing to – well, he didn't know where. There was no way he could escape as traffic was speeding by on either side of him. He found it very difficult to hold on as the wind was getting stronger.

After some manoeuvring he managed to coil his tail around a bit which was sticking out and stabilise himself. The truck didn't stop except at traffic lights. Al was feeling very hungry and kept hoping the driver would stop for something to eat. Then he realised the driver had food with him, because he kept throwing bits of sandwiches, banana skins and apple cores out the window. Al would get a whiff of coffee whenever the window opened.

Al saw signs for Perth and Edinburgh. He realised he was in Scotland, heading for the Highlands. He was grateful for the geography lessons he'd had in school, even if he'd found them a bit boring at the time.

The scenery was certainly beautiful. Al spotted some red deer on the hills and a buzzard circling near the roadway. Further on, he could see snow on the mountains and feel the icy-cold winds. The juggernaut finally stopped at the side of the road. The driver got out and had a stretch and a big yawn.

"About time," said Al.

"Who said that?" the driver asked. Looking around, he could see no one. Since most of the traffic was gone, the driver had the road to himself. He thought the voice he heard was a trick of the wind blowing through the heather.

"Don't throw a wobbly," said Al. "But I'm a hitch-hiker; a reluctant one mind, you, but a hitch-hiker nevertheless." The driver sneaked around the truck to see where the hitch-hiker was hiding, but couldn't see anyone. Then he opened the doors at the back – no one appeared to be hiding inside. He scratched his head and turned around, only to find himself face to face with a snake. "Hi," said Al, beaming broadly. The driver yelled and ran up the road shouting, "Help! Help!"

Al waited until the driver finally came back. He was trembling and had a large stick in his hands. Al hid behind a boulder. The driver searched under and over the truck but could not find him. Eventually, he found the note Al had pinned to the steering wheel.

Listen, sorry for scaring you. I'm Al, an anaconda. I'm friendly, honest. Look to your left.

The driver turned nervously to his left. Al was waving his tail and smiling from the rock.

"Greetings," said Al. "Sorry again for scaring you. I was wondering, do you have a bite to eat? I'm as hungry as a hunter."

The driver threw him an apple which Al caught in his mouth and swallowed whole.

"Delicious," he exclaimed.

The driver became more relaxed and

invited Al to continue the journey inside the truck. Soon they were on first-name terms, Billy the driver and Al the anaconda. Al discovered the driver was a film buff as well, and his favourite films were Westerns. So they had a great chat about films and actors they liked. John Wayne, James Stewart, Clint Eastwood, Audie Murphy and Lee Marvin were high on both their lists of favourites.

After a time, the driver stopped at a roadside restaurant. "Are you hungry?" asked Billy.

"Hungry? I'm starving," said Al. "Plaice and chips would go down very nicely, followed by apple pie and ice cream and a mug of tea."

"You're on," said Billy, who was delighted with the company. He was only sorry Al had spent most of the long journey from London on top of the truck instead of in it. Still, the chat certainly shortened the remainder of the journey for him. As he pulled into the depot near Loch Ness to unload, Al thanked him for the meal and the lift and said his farewell.

Al moved off down the lonely roads. There was no sign of a car. Maybe he should have waited to see if Billy was going back to London after his delivery so he could get a lift. Well, it was too late now. Besides, he'd always fancied visiting Scotland.

Al stopped to admire the moon reflecting in the beautiful loch. The water looked so calm and still. He got the urge to swim so, pulling off the old clothes he was wearing he slipped into the dark waters. It was icy cold, but felt most refreshing. It was very exciting to be back in water; it reminded him of the rivers he used to swim in around Dublin.

After swimming for some time Al

became very sleepy, so he curled himself on a rock on the far side of the loch and slept. Early next morning he awoke. The morning was cold. There was a mist on the loch that made it impossible to see to the far side. A goosander broke the still waters and swam about, but when it saw Al it hurried away. Al decided to have a morning dip and in he went again. It was wonderful. Up and down he moved, twisting and turning from side to side in the brackish water.

Through the mist he saw two men on the other side of the loch. Al waved at them. One of the men dropped his fishing-rod, ran to his Jeep which was parked nearby, and sped away. Al swam up the loch to a monastery where a nice old lady was throwing bread to the ducks and the swans. He submerged himself completely and then popped up in between the water birds. He opened his mouth wide and managed to catch several bits of bread. The ducks were not amused. They quacked and flapped furiously and made circles in the water, then pecked Al on the head.

"Don't be greedy," said the old woman. "There's enough for everyone."

The two swans hissed at Al and swam away, holding their bodies in a threatening position. Even with their threat displays, Al thought they looked very beautiful. He slipped away, leaving the mallards fighting over the last few crumbs. He certainly wasn't full but the few bits of white bread had been delicious.

Moving back to where he first entered the loch, he was astonished to discover the shore lined with people holding cameras, binoculars and telescopes. There were even TV cameras, as well as buses, vans and cars with people hanging out of windows and standing on the roofs of the vehicles. Al moved closer to see what all the fuss was about. Perhaps they were making a film, he thought to himself.

Then there were loud screams and shrieks as people pointed fingers. "There! Over there!" Women screamed and men shouted with excitement. "It's Nessie! the Loch Ness monster."

"Oh no," said Al. "I must be in Loch Ness! I'm out of here! I don't want to be breakfast for any Loch Ness monster." Al twisted and turned but could not see the creature in the dark waters. "It's probably going to attack me from below," Al panicked.

"Did you see the humps?" one spectator yelled.

Al felt something biting his tail. He swam towards the people. "Help!" yelled Al. "I'm being attacked by the Loch Ness monster"

As he got closer to the people he saw a man with a rifle taking aim. The crowds began to scatter. Al heard a loud shout and a bullet whizzed over his head. "Hey, wait a minute," said Al, realising they were shooting at him. "I'm an anaconda," yelled Al. "I'm from a place called Drumcondra, right?"

Another shot rang out that was too close for comfort. He decided it might be better to head for the far side of the loch, hoping he wasn't going to be gobbled up by some prehistoric creature on the way. "What a fine mess I'm in," he sighed. "Men trying to shoot me on the land and a monster trying to eat me in the water. Sometimes it just doesn't pay to get up in the morning."

"There it goes!" yelled someone.

Al swam as fast as he could to get to the far

shore. He was panting hard. "One could lose weight at this game," he grumbled. "Still, there's no sign of that Loch Ness monster." He gave a sigh of relief as he neared the far shore. Then, crash, he bumped into something just below the surface. Al closed his eyes, expecting the worst. He opened one eye and he was face to face with a dog otter.

"I do beg your pardon," said the otter. "Ye see, I thought you were a wee eel, that's why I sank my teeth into you."

"It was you?" said Al, very relieved that it wasn't the Loch Ness monster. "Well, I'm not a wee anything," said Al. "I'm a rather large anaconda, and still growing."

"You're very welcome to these parts," said the otter. "I've never seen anything like you before."

"Well, take a last look – I'm out of here."

"Here," said the otter. "Follow me to my holt and I'll give you some fresh fish."

"Lead the way. Fresh fish!" cried Al with delight as he followed. They moved on to land then across some fields to a river. "This is a grand spot," said Al.

The otter disappeared, then came out of his holt with a fish.

"It's raw," said Al.

"Well, what do you expect?"

"I usually have my fish fried with some batter on it. Don't suppose you have any chips?" The otter looked blank. "No, I suppose not. Well, I'd better get used to it if I'm going bush." The otter still had a blank expression. "I mean, living in the wild, 'back to nature' stuff."

"Oh yes," said the otter. "I see what you mean."

Al knew he didn't, but it was kind of him to share his food and to let him rest in his holt. Meanwhile, helicopters circled overhead and boats drove up and down the loch with camera crews on board, trying to glimpse the Loch Ness monster.

Without any luck.

Next morning, Al said goodbye to the otter and headed downriver, not knowing where it might lead. But, as long as it was far away from Loch Ness, he was content. After visiting various lakes and streams, he eventually found himself in the river Spey near the Cairngorm Mountains. He was really enjoying himself and there were always things to see. Herons, dippers, kingfishers, swans, cormorants and lots of fish which he didn't bother and they didn't bother him. He was a bit wary of anglers so he always swam underwater when he saw them. Thankfully, they never noticed him.

He came to a very quiet stretch of the river and checked up and down. No sign of anglers, or anything else for that matter. He pulled himself out of the water and curled around a large rock for a nap.

"Good heavens! An anaconda," said a

sweet voice. "What on earth are you doing here? Lost, no doubt!"

Al opened his sleepy eyes to see a beautiful young girl with red hair and a big, friendly smile. She didn't seem scared at all of him. Al wondered why. Since he had grown a good bit in recent months most people's first reaction had been to run from him.

"You poor thing. Abandoned, lost and hungry, I suppose?" Al nodded his head. She put her finger on his nose. "I think you understand what I'm saying." Al nodded again. The young girl looked amazed. She lifted Al up from the rock. "My, you are heavy, but very handsome," she declared, putting him around her neck. Al blushed, but the girl didn't notice.

She carried him across the blanket bog to her house. It reminded Al of the times when Fred the Ted would bring him to the cinema, but Fred was no beauty, while this young girl was gorgeous. She lived on a small farm with her mother. Cats and dogs came out to greet her, but they were none too pleased to see the snake. The dog barked furiously and the cats hissed.

"Don't be jealous, we have a visitor who's lost, cold and hungry and we are going to care for it. Like we do with any lost or injured animal we find."

Moira's mother was used to her daughter bringing in lost or injured buzzards, kestrels, owls, foxes, hedgehogs, roe deer and other wildfolk, but she was completely taken by surprise when she saw the snake.

"I don't mind you bringing the snake home," she said anxiously, "but I don't want it in the house."

That suited Moira fine, for she had a mobile home which she'd converted into a studio and sleeping quarters. Moira brought Al to the studio and laid him on the bed. "You're a long way from home! I wonder how you found your way to north

Aviemore?" She stroked him tenderly. "How could anyone abandon you like that?" she said, getting annoyed at the idea.

"Wow!" said Al. "Those paintings are wonderful. Did you paint them?"

Moira couldn't believe her ears. She looked at the snake with her hands on her hips. "Did I just hear you talking?"

Al put on a sheepish expression, then said very softly, "Yes, Moira. That is your name, isn't it?"

The girl sat down on a stool. "I can't believe it. Say something else."

"Any chance of a cup of tea with some toast? And if you had some strawberry jam, it would be smashing."

Moira was astounded. She picked up Al and gave him a hug. "Don't move, I'll be right back with your tea and toast."

Al had no intention of moving; he felt in heaven, on a soft bed away from the cold winds and people trying to catch or shoot him.

Moira hurried back with cake, toast, jam and tea. She picked up her sketch pad. "Do you mind if I sketch you?"

"Sure," said Al, looking at the lovely paintings of tawny owls on the wall. When Moira finished she told Al what a wonderful model he was, keeping so still. He was pleased, and when he saw the pencil sketches of himself he was doubly pleased. Some day those sketches will be in an exhibition, he thought, and people would see how handsome he really was.

Moira's mother called them for dinner and allowed Al to join them. Al's luck had changed. Things couldn't be better: good food, good company, and a warm fire glowing brightly in the hearth. The dogs and cats reluctantly accepted Al's presence. They sat at Moira's feet getting nice titbits from her. The way Al ate, they knew it was a waste of time trying to persuade him to part with any of his meal.

When Moira's mother got used to Al being there, chatting, she decided to ask him a few personal things, like where he was from.

"From Drumcondra, Mam, it's in Dublin."

"But there are no snakes in Ireland," she insisted. "Here in Scotland we have grass snakes, adders and slowworms, but Ireland has no snakes. Of that I am certain."

"Well, I know St Patrick got rid of the snakes," said Al. "But there must have been a few hiding somewhere. How do you explain me? I'm a true Dubliner, no doubt about that. You can tell by my accent. And a true-blue snake as well. Well, more greenish-brown, but you know what I mean."

Moira stroked Al along the neck. "Mum is right. There are no snakes in Ireland, there never were. And certainly not anacondas."

Al was quite shocked. "No snakes in Ireland! Never!"

"I'm afraid not," said Moira.

"Well, that's enough to put one off one's food, that kind of revelation." Then he looked at the dessert. "Pavlova! Mmm! Delicious," he exclaimed. Moira laughed and cut him a large wedge. "Maybe I'm an alien," said Al. "Dropped one night from a UFO."

"I don't think so," laughed Moira. "More likely a truck. A lot of wildlife smuggling goes on around the world. You could be a victim of it."

Al had vague memories of someone saying he was off the back of a lorry. The jigsaw was beginning to fit, he thought. He told them how he went to a movie once about the Swiss Family Robinson and there was this giant snake trying to make a meal out of the family. "It was an anaconda!" He began to panic. "I hope I'm not going to turn out like that."

"Don't mind those films," said Moira's

mother. "They have to make things dramatic like that for the sake of entertainment."

Al remembered saying something exactly like that to Fred the Ted after they saw the film.

After dinner, they all sat down to watch TV. As luck would have it, a wildlife programme called *The Mysteries of the Amazon* was showing. Al sat, wide-eyed, staring at the magnificent jungles, wild animals and colourful birds. Then he saw a beautiful snake sliding down from a tall tree and slipping into a crystal pool. "That's an anaconda," he yelled.

"A female," said Moira.

"Wow, she's gorgeous!" said Al.

When the programme was over, Al asked Moira did she really think he came from such a beautiful place?

Moira nodded, "Yes, definitely."

"I'm not saying Dublin, London or Aviemore aren't beautiful; they are, in their own special way. But those tropical

rainforests we've just seen are magic," said
Al, filled with awe and a strange new longing.

Moira was pleased that Al had
discovered his roots. That night, he went to
sleep and dreamed about the enchanting
place where all those exciting creatures on
the TV roamed free.

Over the next few weeks, Moira got to
know Al really well and did several
paintings and sketches of him.

He enjoyed himself in his new home,
watching crested tits come every morning
to feed on the nuts which hung just outside
the studio. A roe deer nibbled on the small

bushes in the garden and a buzzard circled high over the hills.

Moira, too, was delighted with this very unusual pet. She was tempted to phone the zoo in Edinburgh and ask them if they wanted him, or a travelling circus that was shortly to visit Aviemore. Yet she knew Al was such a freedom-loving snake, she didn't like the idea of him being confined in a glass case or worse.

She knew, however, that she couldn't keep him permanently. Sometimes, she noticed Al had a faraway look in his eyes. When she said "a penny for your thoughts," Al always mentioned the beautiful place he'd seen on the TV programme.

Moira decided it was up to her to do something. She phoned a friend named Grant, who worked at the BBC Natural History Unit, and asked him how would he like to get some good film footage of the elusive anaconda snake.

Grant said he'd love that, but no one had managed to get anything more than a fleeting glimpse of those creatures despite weeks spent waiting for the shots. Moira explained she'd come across an anaconda, and that he would agree to appear in a wildlife film if Grant would transport him back to the Amazon.

Grant laughed loudly. "You're such a kidder, Moira. The snake would 'agree to be filmed' . . . that's good, all right." He laughed even louder.

Moira explained she was very serious and would guarantee the full co-operation of Al, the anaconda. Grant knew Moira had rescued other wild creatures before. Perhaps she really had one, but how on earth had she come across it in Scotland?

Moira added, "By the way, Grant, Al can talk. Would you like to speak with him?"

"Put the anaconda on the phone," said Grant in amazed tones.

Moira called Al. "Will you speak to the wildlife film producer, please?"

"Hello. I'm Al, the anaconda from Drumcondra in Dublin, presently living in north Aviemore, Scotland." There was silence on the other end of the phone, then Al heard a crashing noise.

"Hello? Moira, hello?"

Al handed the phone to Moira. Another member of the unit was on the line. Moira took the receiver. "I don't know what you said to Grant, Moira, but he's just fainted," said the researcher.

"Oops," said Al. "I guess I blew it. They'll never ask me to appear on a film now."

Two days later, the film crew came to visit Moira and Al. Grant had to see this anaconda for himself. He and the crew were very impressed and agreed to fly him to Brazil. Moira and her mom were also invited, which pleased Al.

Al really enjoyed travelling by plane,

looking down on the clouds. He felt like a bird, he said. From the airport they were driven by Jeep to the Amazon basin. Al was released into the jungle. He was very good on camera. They got him swimming, climbing, slithering, crawling and resting.

"Great stuff!" said the director. "You're a true performer."

"I hope you got plenty of close-ups," said Al. "After this film, they might call me the Marlon Brando of wildlife films."

The crew laughed loudly, then something moved in the undergrowth. The camera kept rolling. Suddenly a jaguar appeared, growling and snarling. Everybody trembled, including Al. The big cat came closer to Al, ready to spring into attack. Al stretched himself up to his full size and pushed his body forward until he was nose to nose with the jaguar.

"Listen," said Al. "We can play this two ways . . . one, you go your way and I'll go mine . . . or two, if you mess with me then I'll mess with you. Your choice, buster!" They were locked in eye contact.

Slowly the jaguar backed away. "It's a big forest, there's room enough for everyone," said the jaguar nervously.

"Smart cat!" said Al.

The jaguar turned on its heels and hurried away. The camera crew cheered and applauded Al.

"You certainly stood up to him," said Moira.

"It's all bluff," said Al. "I have to admit I nearly jumped out of my skin when I saw it. Still, it pays to watch old gangster movies.

They teach you how to stand up to bullies . . .
I remember a scene like that with Victor
Mature and Richard Widmark, the film was
Kiss of Death. It was a classic."

"You're a classic," said Moira, giving
him a hug.

Soon it was time for Moira and the film
crew to go. They thanked Al for all his help
and said they were going to title the
documentary *Return to the Wild.* That
sounded just fine to Al.

With tear-filled eyes, he gave them all a
hug. All at the same time.

"Don't squeeze too tightly," said Grant
jokingly. Al waved his tail and made a heart
shape with his body as they headed by Jeep
down the dirt-track. Shafts of warm
afternoon sun slanted through the jungle. Al
yawned and stretched, then decided to have a
rest after all that performing for the cameras.
He'd love to have seen the film, but there
was no chance of a TV around here.

Just as he was about to coil up, he saw a

movement above in the tree canopy. Down
the tree trunk came the most divine creature
Al had even seen. She swung out from the
trunk like a large branch.

"Hello, handsome," said a beautiful voice.
"You're new around these parts." Al was
smitten. Cupid had shot his arrow and hit
Al smack in the centre of his heart. They
intertwined in a friendly fashion. "Fancy a
swim in the river?" asked the female
anaconda. "Or are you too tired from all
that showing off!" She grinned.

"Me? Tired?" said Al. "There's nothing
I'd fancy more than a nice cool dip."

The two of them slithered away towards the Amazon river.

"Hey, Da, come quickly!"

Fred put down the newspaper and followed his son, Mark, into the sitting-room.

"Look, Da, there's a deadly wildlife film on, all about snakes. Didn't you say you once had a pet snake?"

Fred sat down to watch the programme. He couldn't believe his eyes. When he saw Al there on the screen, there was just no mistaking him. He was a lot bigger now, but he was still the old Al he once knew. He called to his wife, who was getting their baby girl, Amanda, ready for bed.

"Quick, hurry!"

Teresa hurried in, carrying the baby. "What's up?"

"Look," he said excitedly. "It's my ol' pal. He's a TV star! Al, the anaconda from Drumcondra."

110